DEAR PEN PAL

By Betsy Franco

Illustrated by Itsuko Tomonari

Macmillan McGraw-Hill
New York Farmington

Dear Pery,

I live in Cleveland. You are my new pen pal.

My teacher said I have to write. I said I didn't want to write to a boy, but she said I should.

How many brothers and sisters do you have? I have one big sister.

Your pen pal,
Susie

Dear Susie,

You're my first pen pal. My teacher says we have to write, too.

I live in Rio in Brazil. I have two sisters and two brothers.

It's almost time for a special holiday here. We dress up and dance all night. It's like a huge party in the street.

Your pen pal,
Pery

Dear Pery,

I liked the stamp on your envelope. I collect stamps.

There is no special holiday here right now. There is just school.

I've never stayed up all night. I wish I could go to Brazil.

Your pen pal,
Susie

P.S. Please send a picture. Here's one of me and my fish.

Dear Susie,

I wish you could come to Brazil, too. Your fish looks nice.

Here is a picture of me at a soccer game. Brazil is great at soccer. We're the best in the world!

Your pen pal,
Pery

Dear Pery,

I went to the store to buy you baseball cards. Cleveland is very good at baseball.

We went to the lake this weekend. It had lots of ice on it. We built a big snowman.

Your pen pal,
Susie

Dear Susie,

You're so lucky! We never have snow! Last week, we went to the beach. The sand is very white. I like to ride the waves with my brothers and sisters. I sent you some sand in a bag. I hope it gets there!

Your pen pal,

Pery

P.S. Thanks for the baseball cards!

Dear Pery,

I loved the sand.
I'd send you some
snow, but it would
melt by the time
you got it.

My teacher says
Brazil has rain
forests. She says
an animal that
looks like a huge
guinea pig lives
there. Do you live
near the rain
forest?

Your pen pal,

Susie

Dear Susie,

I have never been to the rain forest. I live in the city!

My mother says I can invite you to Brazil. Can you come?

Your pen pal,

Pery

Dear Pery,

I wish I could visit you. But Brazil is too far away! I've never even been on a plane!

Maybe we can just keep writing. My teacher says the year is almost over. She says we don't have to write anymore. But I think it's fun to write, even if you are a boy.

Your pen pal,
Susie

Dear Susie,

I think it's fun, too, even if you are a girl. Let's just keep writing. You're the best pen pal I ever had.

Your pen pal,
Pery

Dear Pery,

I'm the only pen pal you ever had, silly! Write to me soon!

Your pen pal,
Susie